BIG stickers
for little hands

EARLY
LEARNING

make
believe
ideas

What's inside?

This activity book is split into four sections. Turn to each new section to discover new early learning topics.

ABC **123** **COLORS AND SHAPES** **ANIMALS**

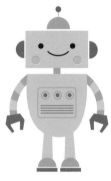

Where there is a missing sticker, you will see an empty shape. Search the sticker pages to find the missing sticker.

There are also card press-outs to make, create, and play with.

1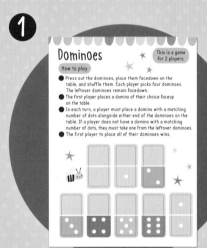

2

3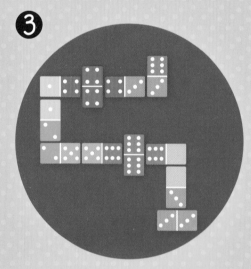

Pull out the card pages at the back of each section.

Gently push the shapes until they pop out.

Follow the instructions to play fun games and complete the puzzles.

Color the **car**.
Use the dots to guide you.

Circle three **dinosaurs**
hiding in the trees.

5

Ee

Circle the object that begins with the letter E on each row.

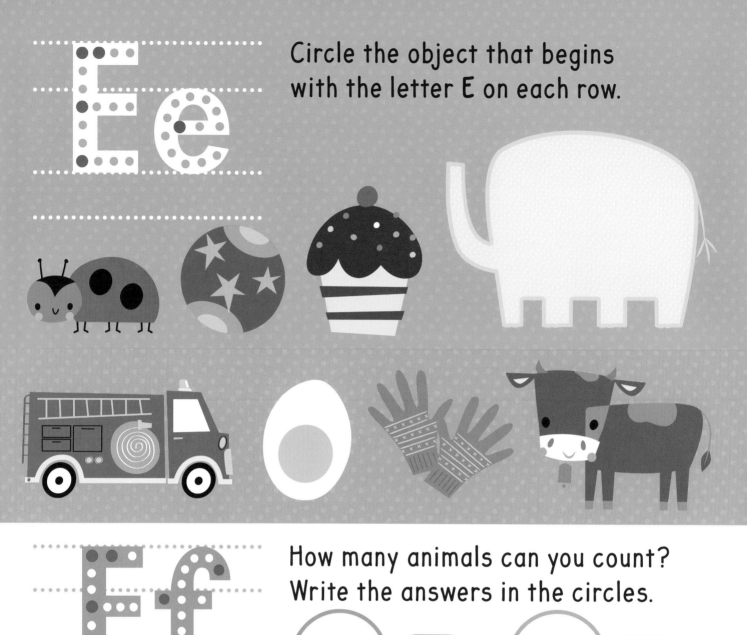

Ff

How many animals can you count? Write the answers in the circles.

frogs

fish

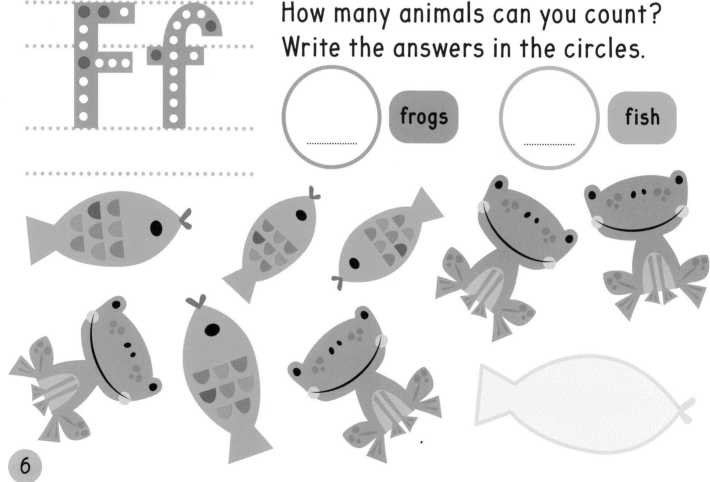

6

G g

Trace the lines to finish the **goose**. Then color it.

H h

Draw lines to match the pairs of **hats**.

Ii

Follow the lines to see who gets the **ice-cream cone**.

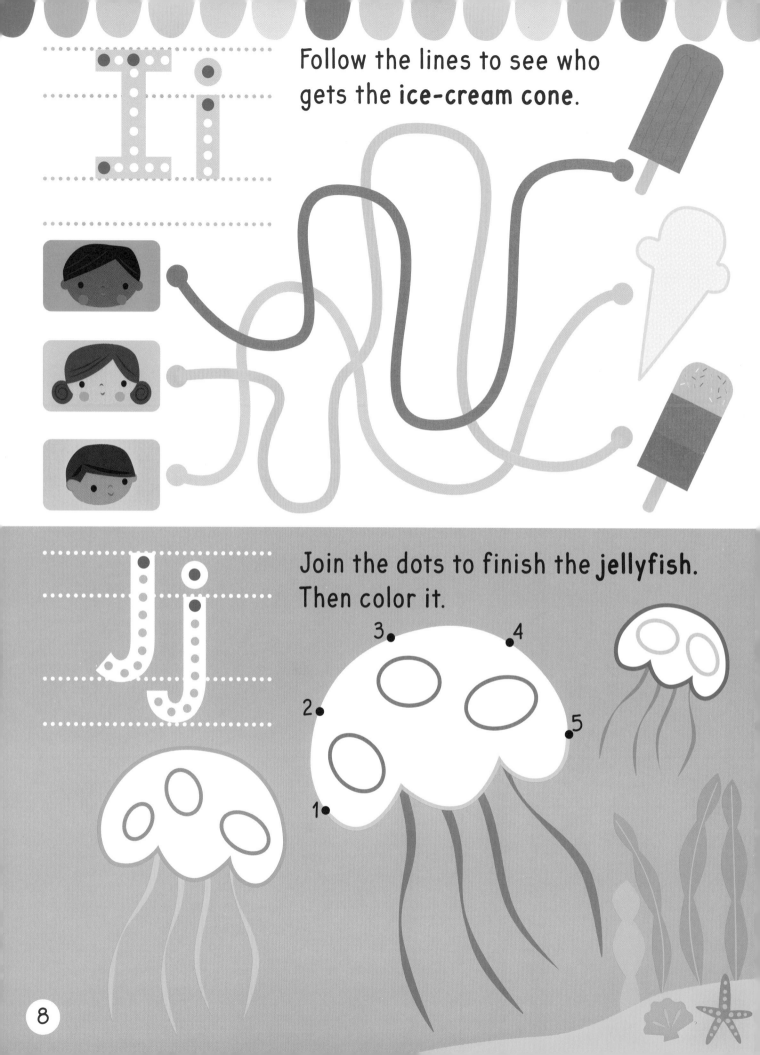

Jj

Join the dots to finish the **jellyfish**. Then color it.

3 •   4 •

2 •

• 5

1 •

Kk

Find and circle three objects that begin with the letter K.

Ll

Unscramble the words that begin with the letter L. Use the pictures to guide you.

l f a e

_ e a _

n o i l

_ i o _

Mm

Draw a line from the objects that begin with the letter **M** to the **M**. The first one has been done for you.

Nn

Use color to finish the pattern on each **necklace**.

Oo

Trace the lines to finish the **orangutan**. Then color it.

Pp

Circle two **parrots** that match.

Qq

Point to the **queen** wearing a red crown.

Rr

Count the objects in each group. Circle the answer.

rockets

1   2   3   4   5

robots

1   2   3   4   5

Ss

Trace the check mark next to the objects that begin with the letter S.

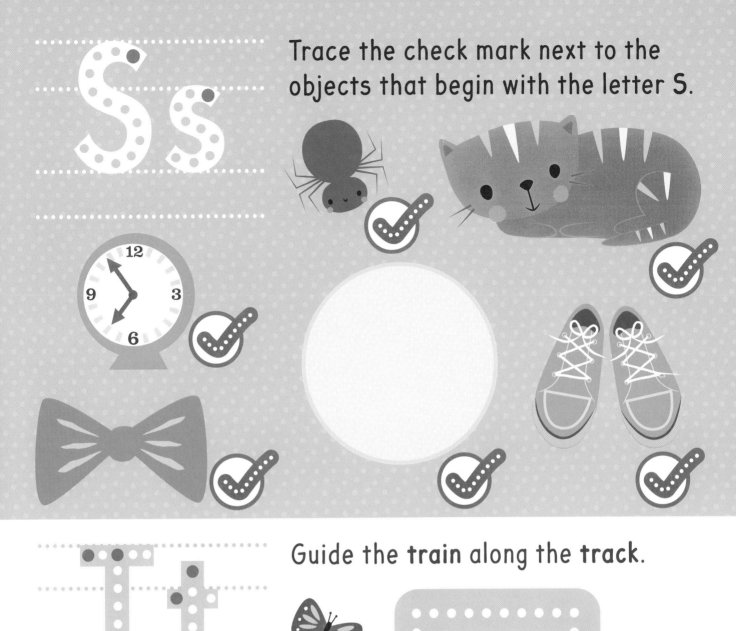

Tt

Guide the **train** along the **track**.

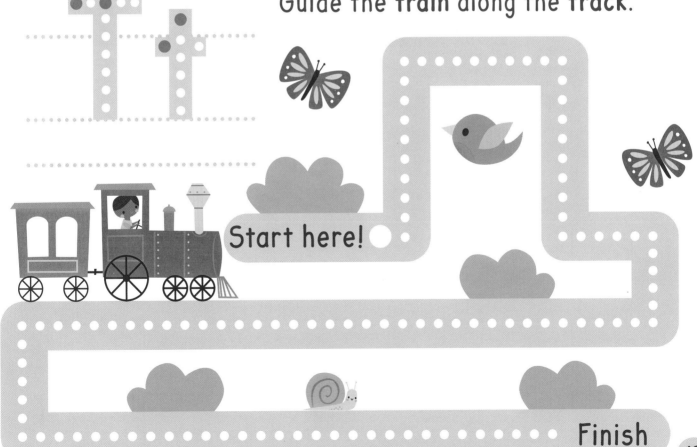

Start here!

Finish

U u

Color the **unicorn**.

V v

Sticker to finish the pattern of **vegetables** on each row.

Look at the **watch**.
Then trace the numbers
to reveal the time.

Color the **xylophone**.
Use the dots to guide you.

15

Circle the **yellow** object on each row.

Find three differences between the **zebras**.

Alphabet bingo

This is a game for 2 players.

How to play:

1 Press out the bingo boards and the letter cards. Place the letter cards facedown on the table and give each player a bingo board.

2 Each player takes it in turns to turn over a letter card. If it matches a letter on their bingo board, they must place the letter card on the bingo board. If the letter card doesn't match, the player must return the letter card, facedown, on the table.

3 The first player to find all the letter cards for their bingo board, shouts "Bingo!" and wins the game.

bingo board

letter card

Extra stickers

Stickers for pages 4–5

Pages 6–7

Pages 8–9

Pages 10–11

Pages 12–13

Pages 14–15

Page 16

123

1 one

Color **1** snail.

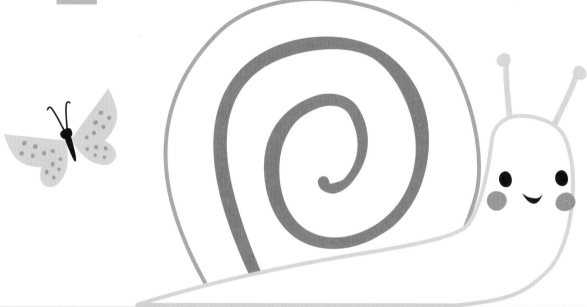

Circle the ladybug with **1** spot.

Circle 2 frogs that match.

3 three

Circle **3** differences between the scenes.

28 Sticker the star when you have finished and say, "I did it!"

4 four

Follow the number 4 to guide the rabbit to the picnic.

Start here! 4   4   4   4   4

4   4

4   3   3   3   4

2   4

2   4   4   4   4   4   4

4

4

4   4   Finish

29

5 five

Trace **5** cars with your finger.

Color and sticker **5** boats.

Number match

Count the objects in each group. Then draw lines to match the groups to the correct numbers.

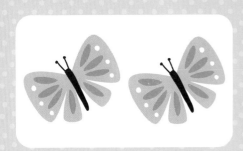

6 six

Circle **6** pigs hiding on the farm.

7 seven

Circle the toybox with 7 toys.

TOYBOX

Color 7 balls.

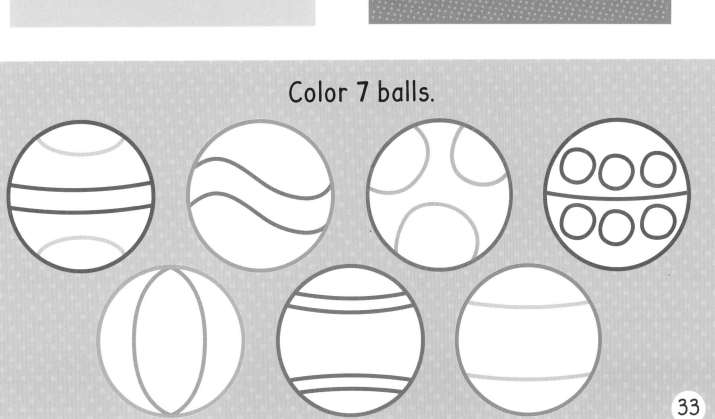

8 eight

Sticker and color to finish the **8** parrots.

Trace the check mark under the tiger with **8** stripes.

9 nine

How many sharks can you count?
Write the answer.

....

10 ten

Join the dots to finish the rocket.
Then count to **10**.

How many stars
can you count?
Write the answer.

....

Number match

Count the objects in each group.
Then draw lines to match the groups
to the correct numbers.

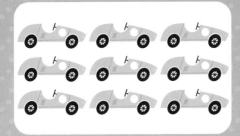

Count and color

Count the dots to work out which color to use in each part of the picture.

- = green   •• = red   ••• = yellow

:: = brown   ⁙ = orange   ⁙: = pink

I spy

Search the picture for the things below. How many can you see? Write the answers in the circles.

....
planes

....
hot-air balloons

....
birds

Number lines

Use the completed number line to help you fill in the missing numbers.

Dominoes

How to play:

1. Press out the dominoes, place them facedown on the table, and shuffle them. Each player picks four dominoes. The leftover dominoes remain facedown.

2. The first player places a domino of their choice faceup on the table.

3. In each turn, a player must place a domino with a matching number of dots alongside either end of the dominoes on the table. If a player does not have a domino with a matching number of dots, they must take one from the leftover dominoes.

4. The first player to place all of their dominoes wins.

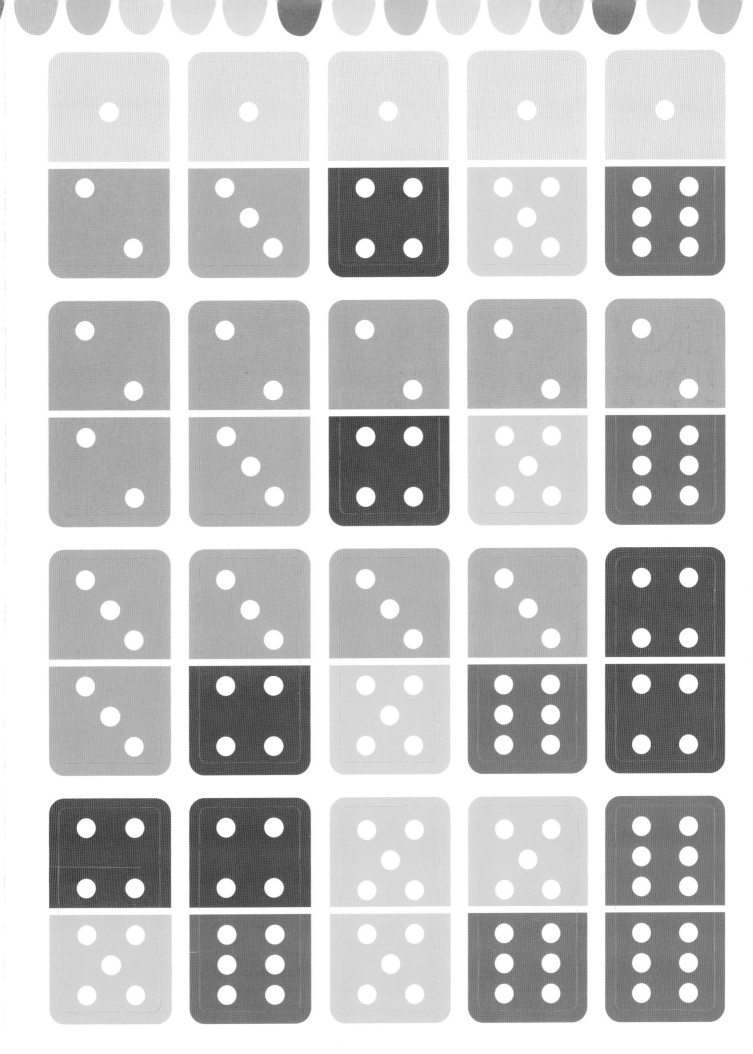

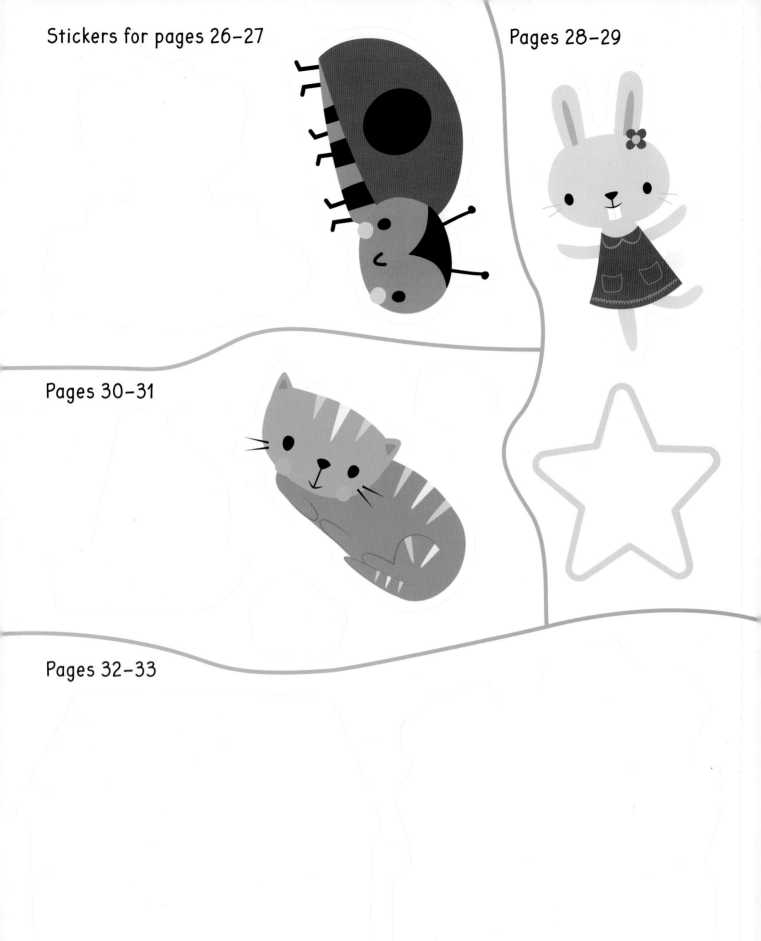

Stickers for pages 26–27

Pages 28–29

Pages 30–31

Pages 32–33

Pages 34-35

Pages 36-37

Pages 38-39

Page 40

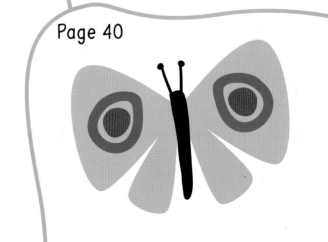

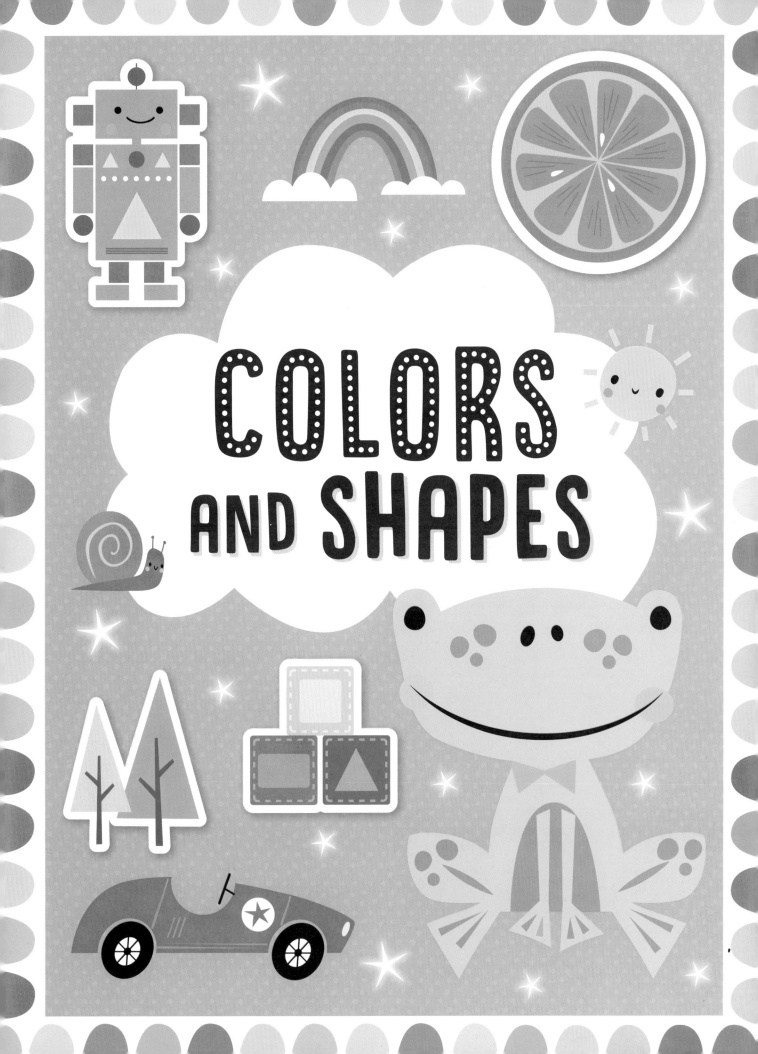

COLORS
AND SHAPES

Red

Color the ladybug in **red**.

Circle three **red** flowers.

Yellow and green

Put a **y** by each **yellow** object.
Put a **g** by each **green** object.
The first one has been done for you.

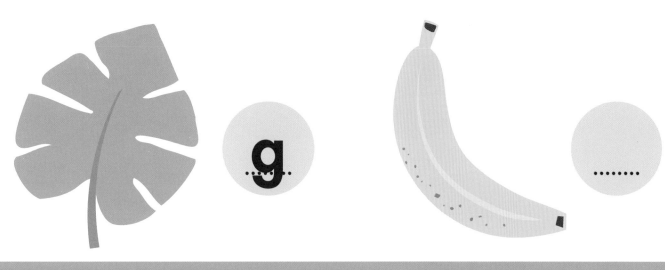

...g...

....

....

....

....

....

Orange

Trace the **orange** things with your finger.

Use a pencil to trace the letters in the word **orange**.

orange

Blue

How many **blue** things can you count?
Write the answer in the circle. ⟶ ....

Pink and purple

Draw a line from the **pink** things to the word **pink**.
The first one has been done for you.

pink

Color the car in **purple**.

Brown

Circle the things that are **brown**.

Black and white

Circle the one that is not
black and white on each row.

Rainbow colors

Color the **rainbow** picture.
Use the dots to guide you.

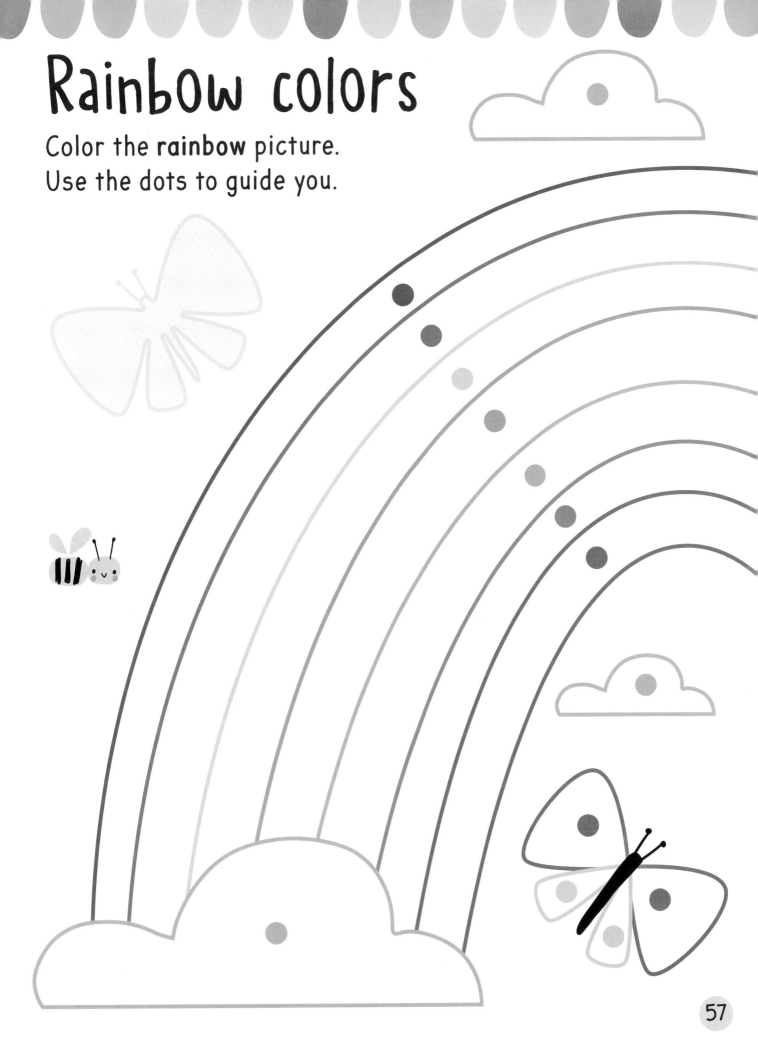

Square

Sticker to finish the pattern of **squares** on each row.

Trace the check mark next to the frame that is **square**.

58

Circle

Point to the objects that are **circular**.

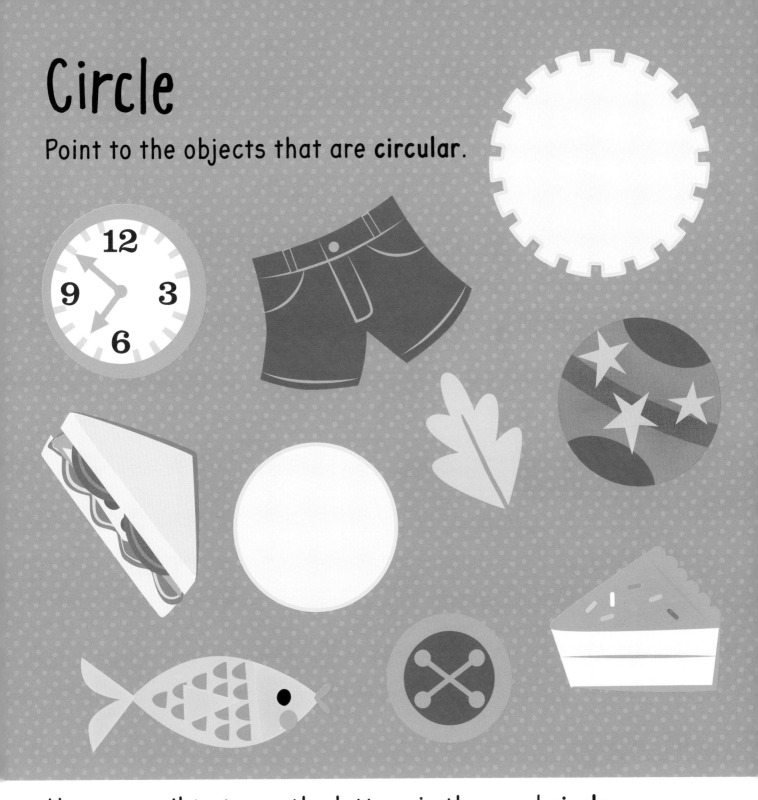

Use a pencil to trace the letters in the word **circle**.

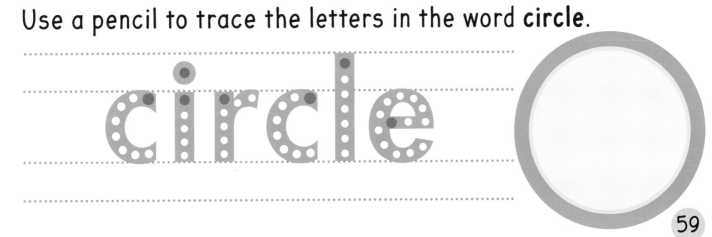

circle

Triangle

Trace the **triangles** in the palace. Then color it.

Find and circle three **triangular** trees.

Rectangle

Follow the **rectangles** through the maze.

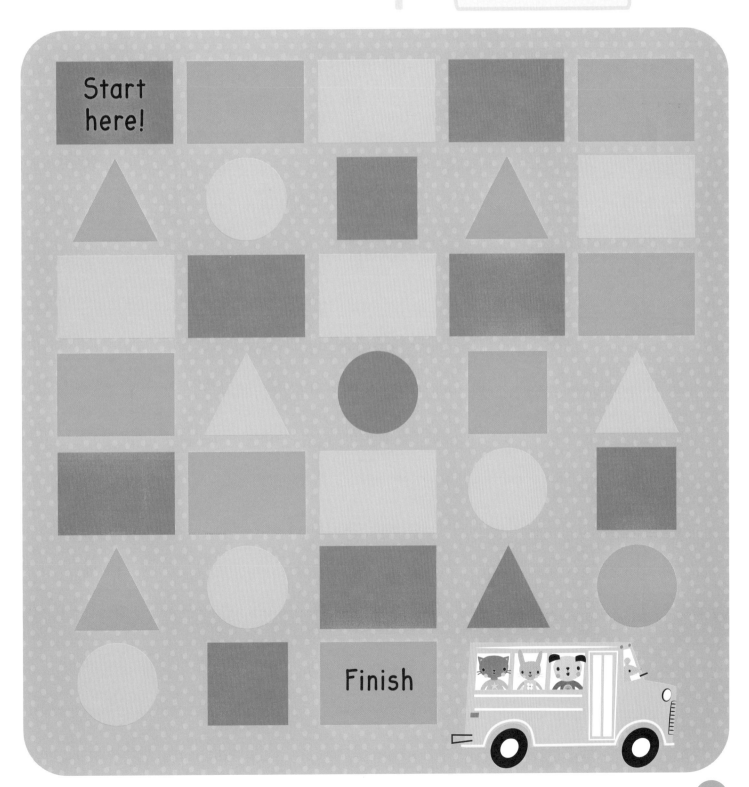

Start here!

Finish

Hearts and stars

How many **hearts** and **stars** can you count?
Write the answers in the circles.

....

hearts   stars

Super shapes

Color the **star**.

Sticker the **square**.

Trace the **circle**.

Color the **heart**.

Colors and shapes

Finish the robot.

Color the...

triangles
in yellow.

rectangles
in blue.

circles
in green.

squares
in red.

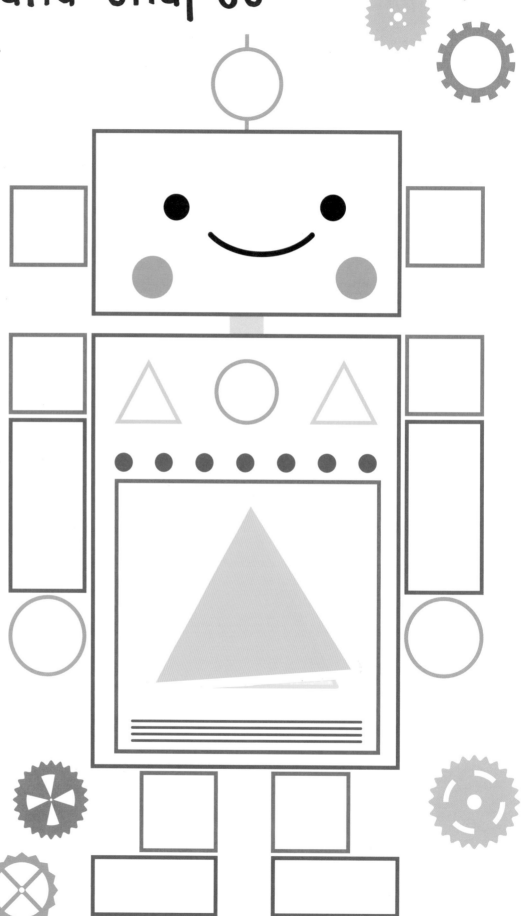

Perfect pairs

How to play:

1 Press out the cards and place them facedown on the table.

2 Turn over two cards at a time. If they match, put them to one side. If they don't, turn them over and try again.

3 Keep going until you've found all the pairs!

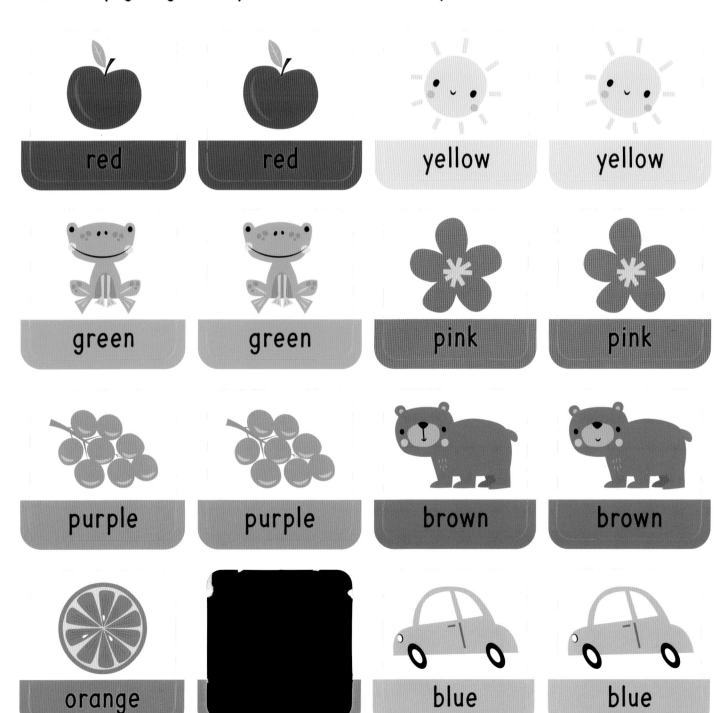

red	red	yellow	yellow
green	green	pink	pink
purple	purple	brown	brown
orange		blue	blue

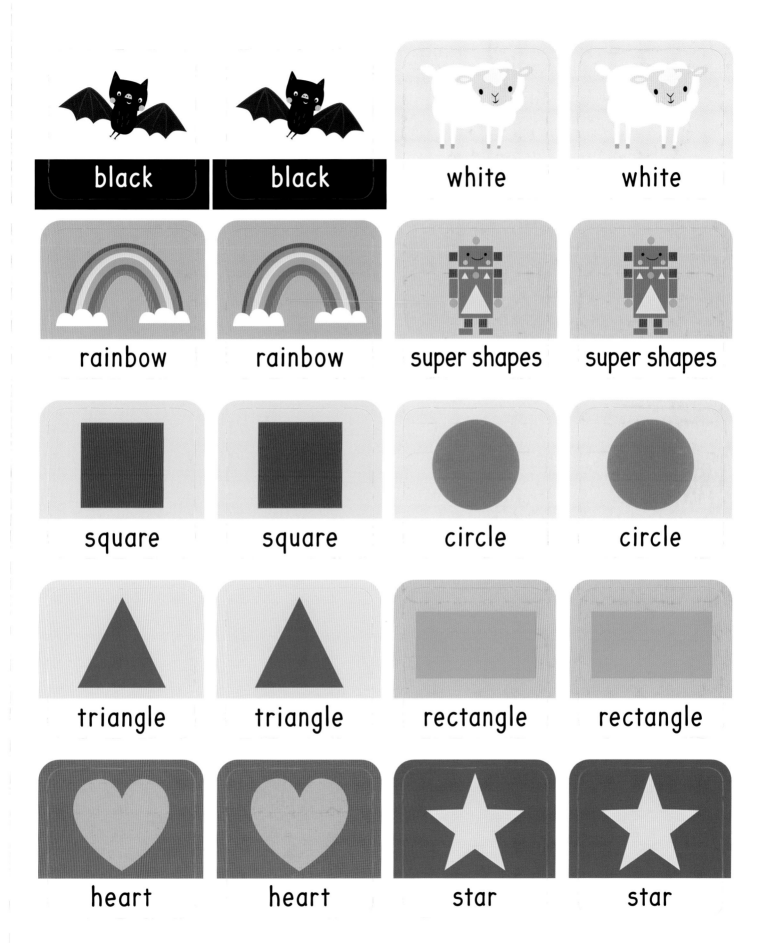

black	black	white	white
rainbow	rainbow	super shapes	super shapes
square	square	circle	circle
triangle	triangle	rectangle	rectangle
heart	heart	star	star

Stickers for pages 50-51

Pages 52-53

Pages 54-55

Pages 56-57

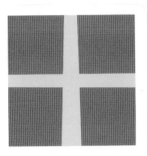

ANIMALS

Happy habitats

Use color and stickers to
discover each animal's habitat.

In the forest

In the desert

In the ocean

In the jungle

Tasty treats

Follow the lines to see what each animal eats.

In the sky

How many of each animal can you count?
Write the answers in the spaces below.

.... birds

.... butterfly

.... bees

Cool colors

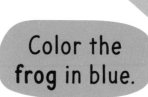

Color the frog in blue.

Color the orangutan in orange.

Sticker the green **chameleon**.

Color the parrot in red.

78

Animal opposites

Draw lines to match the animal opposites.
The first one has been done for you.

slow

awake at night

awake in the day

big

small

fast

Baby animals

Use color and stickers to finish the animals and their babies.

chick

penguin

calf

moose

cub

lion

lamb

sheep

81

What's my name?

Sticker the animal names.

I am a...

I am a...

I am a...

I am a...

82

Pretty patterns

Search the scene for the patterns below.
Trace the check marks as you find them.

spots

stripes

zigzags

Animal sounds

Trace the words to find out what sound each animal makes. Then color and sticker to finish.

tweet

woof

Cute critters

Count the animals to finish the sums.

$$1 \quad + \quad 2 \quad = \quad ....$$

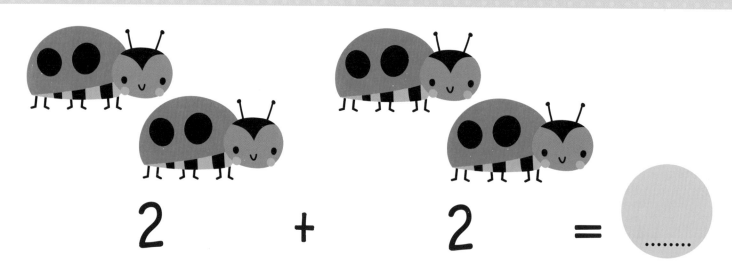

$$2 \quad + \quad 2 \quad = \quad ....$$

$$2 \quad + \quad 3 \quad = \quad ....$$

Find us!

Find and circle three animals that start with the letter f.

At night

Use a pencil to trace the path to the **owl's** nest.

Start here!

How many **bats** can you count? Write the answer. ....

Finish

Animal shapes

Press out the shapes.
Then make these three animals.

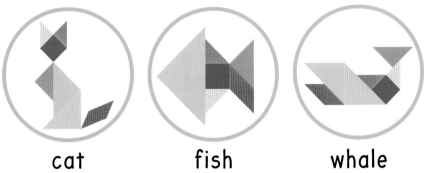

cat   fish   whale

What other animals can you create?

Super stencils

Press out the stencils. Use them to draw your own animals in the book or wherever you like!

Stickers for pages 74–75

Pages 76–77

Pages 78–79

Pages 80–81

Pages 82–83

walrus

Pages 84–85

Pages 86–87

Page 88